Iris and Walter

and Baby Rose

Iris and Walter
and Baby Rose

WRITTEN BY

Elissa Haden Guest

ILLUSTRATED BY

Christine Davenier

sandpiper

Green Light Readers
HOUGHTON MIFFLIN HARCOURT
BOSTON   NEW YORK

For my Gena, with all my love—E.H.G

For Rose Schelameur—C.D.

Text copyright © 2002 by Elissa Haden Guest
Illustrations copyright © 2002 by Christine Davenier

SANDPIPER and the SANDPIPER logo are trademarks of Houghton Mifflin Harcourt Publishing Company.

Green Light Readers and its logo are trademarks of Houghton Mifflin Harcourt Publishing Company, registered in the United States of America and/or its jurisdictions.

For information about permission to reproduce selections from this book, write to trade.permissions@hmhco.com or to Permissions, Houghton Mifflin Harcourt Publishing Company, 3 Park Avenue, 19th Floor, New York, New York 10016.

www.hmhbooks.com

First Green Light Readers edition 2012

The text of this book was set in Fairfield Medium.
The display type was set in Elroy.
The illustrations were created in pen-and-ink on keacolor paper.

The Library of Congress has cataloged the hardcover edition as follows:
Guest, Elissa Haden.
Iris and Walter and Baby Rose/written by Elissa Haden Guest; illustrated by Christine Davenier.
p. cm.
Summary: Iris's baby sister Rose is a very, very fussy baby, and Grandpa takes Iris out for a special day without the baby.
[1. Babies—Fiction. 2. Sisters—Fiction.
3. Sibling rivalry—Fiction. 4. Grandfathers—Fiction.]
I. Davenier, Christine, ill. II. Title.
PZ7.G9375Is 2002
[E]—dc21 2001001381

ISBN: 978-0-15-202120-7 hardcover
ISBN: 978-0-547-85064-1 paperback

Manufactured in China
LEO 20 19 18 17 16 15 14 13 12 11

4500779201

Contents

1. Iris's Big News

One autumn day, Iris's mother said, "Iris, my love, I have some news to tell you. I'm going to have a baby." "Really?" asked Iris.
"Really," said her father.
"You're going to be a big sister."
"Wow!" said Iris. "Wait till I tell Walter."

"Walter, Walter! I'm going
to be a big sister!" Iris shouted.
"Boy," said Walter, "you're lucky."
"We both are," said Iris.

"It's going to be so much fun.
We'll get to push the baby in a carriage.
We'll feed it a bottle.
It will be just like playing with a doll."
"Gosh," said Walter.

Winter came, and Iris and Walter
went sledding.
They rode Rain down quiet snowy paths.
Some nights Grandpa took them skating
under a winter moon.

At home, Iris's parents were busy
getting ready for the new baby.
"When is that baby coming?" asked Iris.
"In the spring, my Iris," said Iris's mother.
"When everything is green, my Iris,"
said Iris's father.

Outside, the snow
was falling and falling.
Iris thought spring
would never come.
But it did.

2. Baby Rose

One spring day, when the wild roses
were in bloom, Baby Rose was born.
"Hooray!" said Iris's father.
"At last," said Iris's mother.
"How wonderful," said Grandpa.
"Oh, she looks just like a little doll!"
said Iris.

But Baby Rose did not act like a little doll.
Baby Rose was very, very, *very* fussy.
"Baby Rose is no fun," said Iris.
"She will be, my Iris," said Iris's mother.
"Give her time, my Iris," said Iris's father.

Baby Rose began to wail and wail and *wail*.
Iris covered her ears.

The next day, Walter came over after school.
"How is Baby Rose?" he asked.
"Horrible," said Iris.
"Cry, cry, cry—that's all she does."
"I think she's cute," said Walter.

Just then, Baby Rose opened her eyes.

Then she opened her mouth.

"Gosh, you're not kidding!" said Walter.
"I didn't know babies could be so loud!"

"Baby Rose hurts my ears," said Iris.
"Hmm. I have an idea," said Walter.
"I'll be right back."

Walter was back in no time.
"Here, Iris, try these earmuffs," he said.
Iris put on Walter's earmuffs.
They felt warm and soft and fluffy.

Now, Baby Rose sounded far, far away.
"Wow, these earmuffs are terrific,"
said Iris. "I'm *never* taking them off."
"Good idea," said Walter.

24

3. Iris's Day Away

There was no getting around it.
Baby Rose was a fusspot.
Day after day, night after night,
Baby Rose cried and fussed.
"Poor Baby Rose," said Iris's
mother, rocking her in her arms.
"Poor little Rosie," said Iris's
father, patting her on the back.

But Iris was fed up.
"Baby Rose is a crabby cake!
I don't want to be *her* big sister!"
she shouted.
Baby Rose cried harder.

"Stop yelling, Iris," said Iris's mother.
"That's way too loud," said Iris's father.
But Iris didn't care.
She stomped outside
and slammed the door.

"Now, now, what's all
the fuss about?" asked Grandpa.
"I'm not fussy—*she's* the fusspot!" said Iris.
"Iris, do you know what you need?"
asked Grandpa.

"A new sister?" asked Iris.
"A day away," said Grandpa.
"Will it be fun?" asked Iris.
"Oh yes," said Grandpa,
"lots and lots and lots of fun."

And Grandpa was right.
Iris and Grandpa spun
round and round
on the Ferris wheel.

They rode the
roller coaster—
once with their
eyes open,
and once with their
eyes closed.

They threw darts.
They won silly prizes.

They had lots and lots and lots of fun.

By the time Iris and Grandpa got home,
the stars were out and Baby Rose
was fast asleep.
"Come here, my Iris," said Iris's mother.
"We've missed you, my Iris," said Iris's father.
Iris curled up between her mother and father.

Her parents read her favorite books.
They told her favorite stories.
They sang her favorite songs.
Iris was warm and cozy in her parents' arms,
and soon she fell fast asleep.
At least for a little while...

4. Baby Rose's Big Sister

Little by little, Baby Rose began to change.
She fussed less and less.
She ate more and more.
She smiled a lot, especially at Iris.
And before Iris knew it, she didn't need
to wear Walter's earmuffs anymore.

One autumn day,
Iris's mother said, "Iris, my love,
why don't you take Baby Rose for a walk?"
"What if she starts crying?" asked Iris.

"Give her a bottle," said Iris's mother.
"Pat her back," said Iris's father.
"Sing her a song," said Grandpa.

"Do you want to go
for a walk, Baby
Rose?" asked Iris.
And Baby Rose
gave Iris a big smile.

So, off they went.
"This is fun," said Iris.

But halfway down the road,
Baby Rose began to cry.
"Help!" said Iris. "What do I do?"

Baby Rose reached for her big sister.

Iris picked her up.
Baby Rose was soft
and warm.
Her head smelled sweet.
"It's okay, Rosie.
I'm here," said Iris.

Iris gave Baby Rose a bottle,
and patted her back,

and sang her a song.

And by the time they got
to Walter's house,
Baby Rose was all smiles.
"Hey, Walter!" called Iris.
"Come play with Baby Rose.
It's *fun* being a big sister."

And it was.
At least *some* of the time.